Sophie's Box

John Prater

CAMBRIDGE
UNIVERSITY PRESS

Sophie found a big box. It had
a funny smell.

A scarecrow jumped out of the box.
He had a big bowl and a spoon.

The scarecrow said, "Hello, Sophie. Will you help me make a lovely big cake?"

"Oh yes!" said Sophie. "Let's make
a lovely big cake."

The scarecrow said, "Let's start with
a bucket of straw.

Now let's add two buckets of green grass.

Next, we'll add three old carrots and
four old apples,

five smelly eggs, and some *very* smelly cheese.

Last of all, we'll mix in some mud."

"This is silly!" said Sophie.

They mixed it up and tipped it out.
"Yuk!" said Sophie. "It's messy *and*
it's smelly!"

"Here's someone who will like our cake,"
said the scarecrow. "Say hello to Gilbert."

Gilbert ate up the whole cake. He ate
every bit of it.

Then Gilbert wiped everything clean with his napkin.

"You're a wonderful cook," said Gilbert.
Sophie said goodbye to them both.

Dad came in. "Will you help me make
a lovely big cake?" he said.